East of the Sun
and
West of the Moon

Peter Christen Asbjørnsen (1812-1885) and Jørgen Engebretsen Moe (1813-1882) were collectors of Norwegian folklore who published *Norske folke-eventyr* (1841-44; "Norwegian Folktales"), a landmark in Norwegian literature that influenced the Norwegian language.

Asbjørnsen, the son of a glazier, and Moe, the son of a rich and highly educated farmer, met as teenagers in 1826, while they were both attending school in the former parish of Norderhov in southern Norway, and became lifelong friends. Independently, both men began collecting folklore and folktales that had survived and developed from Old Norse pagan mythology in the mountain and fjord dialects of Norway, which they decided to pool together and publish jointly.

At the time, the Norwegian literary was influenced heavily by Danish norms, which was unsuitable for national folklore, while the various dialects used by

Norway's oral storytellers were too local. They solved the problem by applying the principles espoused by the Brothers Grimm of using a simple linguistic style in place of dialects, while maintaining the national uniqueness of the folktales.

Some of the tales appeared as early as 1837 and others were published as *Norske folke-eventyr*. Asbjørnsen's vivid prose and Moe's poems recaptured the folk heritage of Norway for the modern age, and by gathering the tales of ghosts and fairies, gods and mountain trolls, they stimulated a revival of interest in Norway's past and further research into folktales and ballads, as well as reawakening a sense of national identity.

Separately, Asbjørnsen published his collection of fairytales entitled *Norske huldreeventyr og folkesagn* (1845-48; "Norwegian Fairy Tales and Folk Legends"), and Moe published his collection of children's stories, *I brønden og i tjærnet* (1851; "In the Well and the Pond").

Asbjørnsen became a zoologist by profession, and in 1856 he studied methods of timber preservation, and later translated Charles Darwin's *Origin of Species* (1860). Moe graduated with a degree in theology, and though his *Digte* (1850; "Poems") placed him among the Norwegian Romantic poets, he was ordained in 1853 after experiencing a religious crisis, and became Bishop of the Diocese of Kristiansand in 1874.

EAST OF THE SUN
AND
WEST OF THE MOON
A Norwegian Folktale

PETER CHRISTEN ASBJØRNSEN
AND
JØRGEN ENGEBRETSEN MOE

*Translated by Margaret Hunt
and George Webbe Dasent
Adapted by Rachel Louise Lawrence*

Blackdown
PUBLICATIONS

This adaption of Peter Christen Asbjørnsen and Jørgen
Engebretsen Moe's *"Østenfor sol og vestenfor måne"* from *'Norske
Folke-Eventyr'* (1841) and *"Kvitebjørn kong Valemon"* from
'Norske Folke-Eventyr: Ny Samling' (1871), and English
translations by Margaret Hunt from Andrew Lang's 'The Blue
Fairy Book' (1889) and George Webbe Dasent from 'Popular
Tales from the Norse' (1859) and 'Tales from the Fjeld' (1874),
first published in 2014 by Blackdown Publications; revised and
extended edition published in 2020

ISBN-13: 978-1520361017

Illustration on front cover by Theodor Kittelsen (1857-1914)

Aarne-Thompson-Uther [ATU] Classification of Folk Tales
II. 300-749: Tales of Magic
> II.ii. 400-459: Supernatural or Enchanted Wife, Husband or
> Other Relative
>> II.ii.ii. 425-449: Husband
>>> II.ii.ii.i. 425: The Search for the Lost Husband
>>>> *II.ii.ii.i.i. A: The Animal as Bridegroom*

CONTENTS

East of the Sun and West of the Moon

A NORWEGIAN FOLKTALE

Chapter One
An Unexpected Visitor

O nce upon a time, there was a peasant who lived in a cottage in the woods with his wife and their many children. But he was poor and had not much to give his children, neither of food nor clothing. All of the children blessed upon him and his wife were beautiful, but the most beautiful was their youngest daughter, whose beauty knew no bounds.

One Thursday evening in late autumn, the weather was wild and rough outside, and it was cruelly dark. The rain was falling so heavily and the wind was blowing so strongly that the walls of the cottage shook. The family was sitting round their meagre fire in the hearth, each busy with some task or other, when all of a sudden something rapped three times on the windowpane.

The father then went out to see what was

going on, thinking the matter must be grave indeed for someone to venture outside during such a storm; and when he got out of doors, what should he see but a great big white bear.

"Good evening to you," said the White Bear, who seemed not to be aware of the violent weather about him.

"Good evening," said the man.

"If you will give me your youngest daughter, I shall make you as rich as you are now poor," said the White Bear.

It would be truly wonderful to be so rich, thought the man. However, he could not agree to such an arrangement without first talking with his daughter.

"I must first ask my daughter about this," he said, and he returned to his family, who remained seated by the fireplace. "A great white bear waits outside," he told them, "and he has promised to make us rich if he can only have our youngest daughter."

Aghast, his youngest daughter cried, "No!"

No words or deeds could get her to say anything else, and so the man went out again. But he did not admit to his daughter's refusal. Instead, he settled with the White Bear that he should come again the next Thursday evening to receive her answer.

Chapter Two
The White Bear's Castle

D uring the week that followed, her family sought to persuade her and they gave her neither peace nor rest. They talked to her so much of the wealth they would have if she agreed to go with the White Bear—telling her what a good thing it would be for her also, and how well off she would be—that she eventually thought better of it and gave in before the week had passed.

Upon making up her mind to go, she washed and mended all her rags, made herself as presentable as she could, and held herself in readiness to set out with the White Bear.

The next Thursday evening, the White Bear came to fetch her, and she walked out to him, with the bundle in which she had secured her few possessions in her hand.

"You have all you wish to bring with you?" he

asked.

"Yes," said the girl. "I have little enough to take away with me."

"Come then."

Once she had seated herself upon his back, her bundle held tightly against her, they departed.

When they had travelled part of the journey, the White Bear asked her, "Are you afraid?"

"No, I am not," she said as she watched the wilderness they passed through with great fascination.

"Well, keep a tight hold of my fur," he said, "and then there is nothing to fear."

And so she rode a long time, travelling a long way, until they came to a great mountain. There, on the face of it, the White Bear knocked, and a door opened.

Walking forward, they entered a castle, where many brilliantly lit rooms shone with gold and silver. One such room was a great hall, in which there was a table already laid, and it was a spread so magnificent that it would be hard to make anyone understand just how magnificent it was.

The White Bear gave her a silver bell and told her, "Whenever you need anything, you need only ring this bell and what you want will appear at once."

After she had eaten the delicacies and drunk the refreshments, and as night drew near, the girl grew sleepy from her journey, and thought, *I would like to go to bed.* So she lifted the beautifully engraved bell and no sooner had she tilted her hand to sound the clapper than she found herself in a chamber, where a bed stood already made up for her. It was as lovely as any bed one could wish to sleep in, with silken pillows and curtains fringed with gold, and all that was in the room was of gold and silver.

But when she had gone to bed and extinguished the light, a man came and lay down beside her. It was the White Bear, who cast off the form of his beastly shape at night; but she never saw him, for he always came to her after she had extinguished the light; and before the light of morning dawned, he was gone again.

Chapter Three
Longing for Home

For a while, all went well and the girl was happy, but after a time, she began to feel sorrowful and grew silent, for all day long she went about alone, and she longed for home and her parents and siblings.

So one day, the White Bear asked, "What is wrong with you? What is it that you want?"

"It is so dull here in the mountain," she told him. "Here, I have only myself for company. At home, in my parents' house, there are all my siblings. It is because I cannot go to my father and mother, my brothers and sisters, that I am so sad."

"There might be a cure for that," said the White Bear, "but you must promise me one thing—never to talk with your mother alone, but only when the others are nearby to hear, for she will take you by the hand and try to lead you into a room to talk with you alone. But you must not do that at all costs, " he continued, "otherwise, you will make us both greatly unhappy."

One Sunday, the White Bear came to her and said, "We can now set out to visit your parents and siblings."

Overjoyed, the girl sat upon his back and they journeyed a great distance. It took a long time, but at last they came to a large white-washed farmhouse. It was all so pretty, it was a pleasure to look at.

"This is where your parents now live," said the White Bear.

Indeed, she saw her brothers and sisters run around the farmhouse, playing out of doors.

As she dismounted, the White Bear said, "Do not forget what I told you, otherwise you will make us both miserable."

"No, indeed," she said, "I shall not forget."

When she reached the farmhouse, the White Bear turned round and went back to his castle.

When she went inside to see her parents, there was such joy, it seemed there was no end to it. Each family member thought, *I can never thank her enough for all she has done for me*, for now they had everything they wanted and everything was as good as it could be.

At length, they all wanted to know how she

was faring and where she was now living.

"Well," she said, "all is well with me too. Where I live is a very good place indeed and I have everything I could wish for." What other answers she gave, I cannot say, but I do not think they got much out of her.

However, in the afternoon, when they had eaten dinner, all happened as the White Bear had said.

"I must talk with you alone," her mother said. "Come, let us go to your chamber."

But she remembered the words of the White Bear and would not go up the stairs for any reason. "What we have to talk about will keep," she said, and put her mother off.

However, somehow or other, her mother got round her in the end and persuaded her to tell the whole story of her life at the White Bear's castle.

At some point in her account, the girl said, "And every night, when I have gone to bed, a man comes and lays down beside me as soon as I have put out the light. And I have never seen him, for he is always up and away before the morning dawns."

She confessed to her mother of how she continually went about full of woe and sorrow, thinking of how she would love to see him. And how, during the day, she went about the castle alone, and it was a dull and solitary existence.

Her mother huffed and said, "It may well be a Troll you lie with! But I shall now teach you a way that you may see him. I shall give you a candle stub, which you can take away with you, hidden in your bosom. Then, when he is asleep, light it to look upon him and view his true form, but take care not to drop any tallow on him."

With some reluctance, the girl accepted the candle stub from her mother and hid it in her bosom, and when the White Bear came in the evening to fetch her away, she bid a fond farewell to her family.

Chapter Four
Truth by Candlelight

When they had travelled some distance on their way back to the castle, the White Bear asked her, "Did everything with your mother happen just as I foretold?"

She thought to deny his words but discovered that she could not.

"Well," said the White Bear, "if you have listened to your mother's advice, then you have brought unhappiness on us both, and all that has passed between us will be over."

"No," she said, "I have not done anything at all."

The White Bear, however, seemed not to take any comfort in her words.

When she reached home and had gone to bed, it went the same as it had every other night she had spent in the castle—a man came and lay down beside her after she had extinguished the light.

But in the dead of night, when she could hear that he was sleeping, she got up and struck a light, lit the candle stub and let the light shine on him. She then saw that he was the most handsome Prince one could ever set eyes upon, and she fell so deeply in love with him that she thought, *I cannot live if I do not kiss him this very moment*. So, she leaned over and kissed him, but in doing so she dropped three hot drops of tallow on his shirt, and he woke up.

"What have you done?" he cried. "Now you have made us both unhappy. If you had held out for this one year, I would have been saved. For I have a stepmother who has bewitched me so that I am a White Bear by day and a Man by night.

"But now all is at an end between us, and I must leave you and go to her. She lives in a castle that lies East of the Sun and West of the Moon, and there too lives a Princess with a nose three ells long, and she is the one I must now marry."

"How was I to know?" the girl lamented as she wept and wailed.

But there was nothing to be done about it; he had to depart.

Then she asked him, "Might I be able to go

with you?"

"No, that can never happen," he said.

"Can you tell me the way, so I can search for you? Surely I may be allowed to do that!" she said.

"Yes, you may do that," he said, "but there is no way that leads to the castle, for it lies East of the Sun and West of the Moon, and you will never find your way there."

Chapter Five
The Search for a Prince

When the girl awoke in the morning, both the Prince and the castle were gone. She lay on a small, green plot of grass in the middle of a dark, dense forest, and beside her lay the same bundle of rags she had brought with her from her old home.

When she had rubbed the sleep from her eyes, and wept until she was weary, she set out on her way, and she walked for many, many days until, at last, she reached a great mountain.

At its base there sat an old woman, playing with a golden apple.

"By chance," the girl asked, "do you know the way to the Prince, who lives with his stepmother in the castle which lies East of the Sun and West of the Moon, and who is to marry a Princess with a nose three ells long?"

"How do you know about the Prince?" asked

the old woman. "Maybe you are the one who should have had him?"

"Yes," she said, "indeed, I am."

"So it *is* you, is it?" said the old woman. "I know nothing about the Prince, other than he lives in a castle which is East of the Sun and West of the Moon. But I do know you will be late getting there, if ever you get there at all.

"Still," she continued, "you may borrow my horse, and you can ride him to an old woman who is a neighbour of mine. Perhaps she can tell you more. When you arrive there, just give the horse a switch under the left ear and bid him to go home again. And you may take this golden apple with you."

The girl accepted the apple and mounted the old woman's horse. She rode for a long, long time until, at last, she came to another mountain, beside which sat another old woman with a golden carding-comb.

The girl greeted the old woman then asked her, "Do you know the way to the castle that is East of the Sun and West of the Moon?"

Like the other old woman, she answered, "I know nothing about it, except it lies East of the Sun and West of the Moon, and you will be late getting there, if ever you get there at all.

"But," she continued, "you too may borrow my

horse to ride to my nearest neighbour. Maybe she knows more. When you get there, just give the horse a switch under the left ear and bid him to go home again."

The old woman then gave her the golden carding-comb, saying, "Perhaps you may find some use for it."

The girl then mounted the horse, and again rode a long, long way until, at long last, she came to a great mountain, beside which sat another old woman spinning with a golden spinning-wheel.

Of this woman, too, the girl asked, "Do you know the way to the Prince, and where to find the castle which lies East of the Sun and West of the Moon?" But her response was only the same thing once again.

"Perhaps you are the one who should have had the Prince?" said the old woman.

"Yes, indeed," said the girl, "I should have been the one."

"I know the way to the Prince no better than the others. And I know the castle lies East of the Sun and West of the Moon, but that is all. I also know," she said, "that you will be late getting there, if ever you get there at all.

"Still, I will lend you my horse, and then I think you had best ride to the East Wind and ask him. Maybe he knows the place and can blow you there. When you reach him, you need only give the horse a switch under the left ear, and he will trot home again."

The old woman then gave her the golden spinning-wheel. "Maybe you will find a use for it," she said.

Now laden with a golden apple, a golden carding-comb, and a golden spinning-wheel, the girl set off to find the East Wind. She had to ride for a great many days, for a long and wearisome time, before she arrived at the East Wind's house.

But, at last, she did reach it, and then she asked the East Wind, "Can you tell me the way to the Prince who lives East of the Sun and West of the Moon?"

"Well," said the East Wind, "I have often heard tell of the Prince, and of the castle, but I do not know the way there, for I have never blown so far. But, if you wish, I will go with you to my brother, the West Wind. Maybe he knows, for he is much stronger than I am. If you will sit on my back, I shall carry you there."

So the girl seated herself on his back and they set off, moving along swiftly and smoothly.

When they got there, they went into the West Wind's house and the East Wind said to his brother, "I have brought with me the girl who should have had the Prince who lives in the castle that is East of the Sun and West of the Moon. She is now travelling far and wide in search of him."

"Why have you come here?" asked the West Wind.

"To learn from you whether you know the whereabouts of the castle."

"No," said the West Wind, "for I have never blown so far. But, if you want, I will go with you to our brother the South Wind, for he is much stronger than either of us, and he has flown far and wide. Perhaps he can tell you what you want to know. Now," he said to the girl, "if you will sit on my back, I will carry you to him."

So this she did, and they travelled to the house of the South Wind, and were not long in the air to get there.

When they arrived, the West Wind asked of his brother, "Can you tell this girl the way to the castle which is East of the Sun and West of the Moon? For she is the one who should have had the Prince who lives there."

"She is the one," said the South Wind. "Is that so?"

"Indeed, I am," said the girl.

"Well," he said, "I have breezed about a great

many places in my time, but I have never blown so far as that. But, if you want, I will take you to my brother the North Wind. He is the oldest and strongest of us all, and if he does not know where it is, you will never find anyone in the world able to tell you. You can sit upon my back and I will carry you there."

So the girl sat upon his back, and he went away from his house in great haste, making the journey a short one. When they came to where the North Wind lived, he was so wild and blustery that they felt his cold gusts long before they reached his house.

"Blast you both, what do you want?" the North Wind howled at them from afar, so powerful that it struck them with an icy shiver.

"Well, you need not bluster so," said the South Wind, "for here I am, your brother, the South Wind, and here is the girl who should have had the Prince that lives in the castle which lies East of the Sun and West of the Moon. And now she wants to ask you if you have ever been there and can tell her the way, for she desires very much to find him again."

"Yes, I know where it is well enough," said the North Wind. "I once blew an aspen leaf there, but I was so tired that I could not summon the strength to blow for many days afterwards. But, if you truly wish to go there, and are not afraid to go with me, I will take you on my back and see if I can blow you there."

"With all my heart," she said, "I want to go there, I must go there, if it is in any way possible. And as for fear, I have none, no matter how madly you go."

"Very well then," said the North Wind, "but you must sleep here tonight, for we must have the whole day before us if we are ever to get there."

Early the next morning, the North Wind woke her, and puffed himself up, and blew himself out, and made himself so big and strong, it was terrifying to look at him. He then carried them up and away through the air, as if they were going directly to the ends of the earth.

Below them, there was such a ferocious storm; it blew down many houses and long tracts of wood, and as they swept over the great sea, it wrecked ships by the hundred.

In this way, they travelled far—so far that no one can believe how far they went—and all the while they travelled over the sea.

The North Wind became more and more weary, and so exhausted and out of breath that he was barely able to blow any longer. He sank lower and lower, until at last he dropped so low that the crest of the waves splashed against the girl's heels.

"Are you afraid?" asked the North Wind.

"No," she said, "I am not;" and it was true.

By now, they were not far from land, and there was just enough strength left in the North Wind that he could throw her onto the shore beneath the windows of the castle that lay East of the Sun and West of the Moon. But then he was so weary and worn out, he had to stay there and rest for many days before he could go home again.

Chapter Six
Access to the Troll Castle

The next morning, the girl sat down beneath the windows of the castle, and began to play with the golden apple; and the first person she saw was the long-nosed Princess who was to have the Prince.

"How much do you want for your golden apple, girl?" she said as she opened a window.

"It is not for sale, not for gold or money," the girl answered.

"If it is not for sale for gold or money, what do you want for it? You may name your price," said the Princess.

"Well, you can have it," said the girl who had come with the North Wind, "if I may come up to the Prince who lives here, and stay with him tonight."

"Yes, you may do that," said the Princess, for she had made up her mind what she would do, and she took possession of the golden apple.

When the girl went up to the Prince's bedroom that night, he was fast asleep. She shouted and shook him, and between times she wept, but she could not wake him, for they had given him a sleeping draught.

The next morning, at first light, the Princess with the long nose came and chased her out of the Prince's room.

Later that day, the girl sat down beneath the windows of the castle once more, and began to card yarn with her golden carding-comb, and all happened as it had before.

The Princess opened a window and asked her, "How much do you want for your carding-comb?"

As before, the girl replied, "It is not for sale, not for gold or money. But if I am allowed to go up to the Prince, and be with him during the night, you can have it."

But when she went up to the Prince's room, she found him fast asleep again, and no matter how much she shouted and shook him, no matter how much she wept and prayed, he slept on, and she could not bring him to life.

When the first light of day appeared, the long-nosed Princess came and, for a second time, chased her out through the door.

As the day wore on, the girl sat down beneath the windows of the castle once again, and began to spin with her golden spinning-wheel, and the Princess with the long nose wanted to have that as well. So she opened a window and asked, "How much do you want for your spinning-wheel?"

As she had twice before, the girl said, "It is not for sale, not for gold or money. But you can have it, if I can come up to the Prince who lives here, and be with him during the night."

"Yes," said the Princess, "you are welcome to do that."

Now, some Christian folk had been brought to the castle, and while they had been sitting in their room—which was next to that of the Prince—they had heard tell of a woman inside, who had been crying and calling out to him for two nights in a row, and they told this to the Prince.

In the evening, when the long-nosed Princess came once more with her sleeping draught, the Prince pretended to drink, but disposed of it behind him, for he suspected it contained a potion meant to induce sleep.

So, when the girl came in, she found the Prince wide awake; and then she told him the whole story of how she came to be there.

"Ah," said the Prince, "you have come just in time, for tomorrow is to be my wedding day. But I do not want to marry the long-nosed Princess, and you are the only one who can save me.

"I will say that I want to see what my bride can do, and ask her to wash the shirt which has the three drops of tallow on it. She will agree, for she does not know that you are the one who let them fall on it.

"But only Christian folk can do such work, not a pack of Trolls, and so I will say that I do not want any other for my bride but the one who can wash them out. Knowing you can do so, I will then ask you to do it."

There was great joy and love between them all that night; and the next day, when the wedding was to take place, the Prince said, "First, I want to see what my bride can do."

"Yes, that you may do," said the old Troll hag, who was stepmother to the Prince.

"I have a fine shirt," said the Prince, "which I want to wear as my wedding shirt, but there are three drops of tallow on it, which I want to have washed off. I have vowed that I will never take any other as my bride but the one who is able to do that. If she cannot, then she is not worth marrying."

"Well, that is a small matter," said the old Troll

hag, and she and her daughter, the Princess with the long nose, agreed to it.

The long-nosed Princess began to wash the shirt as best she could, but the more she washed and scrubbed, the larger the stains grew.

"Oh, you cannot wash at all!" said the old Troll hag. "Let me have it!"

But the old Troll hag had not long taken the shirt in her hands before it became worse than ever, and the more she washed and scrubbed, the bigger and blacker the stains grew.

So then all the other Trolls had to try and wash the shirt. But the longer they persisted, the blacker and uglier the shirt became, until finally the whole of the Prince's shirt looked like it had been up the chimney.

"Oh," cried the Prince, "not one of you is good for anything at all! There is a foundling-girl sitting outside the window, and I am certain that she is much better at washing than any of you. You girl, come in here!" he shouted.

So, the girl came in.

"Can you wash this shirt clean, girl?" he asked.

"Oh, I do not know," she said, "but I will try."

No sooner had she taken the shirt and dipped it in the water than it was as white as snow, and even whiter than that.

"You," said the Prince, "are the girl I will

marry."

At that, the old Troll hag flew into such a rage that she burst. The Princess with the long nose, and all the other Trolls, must have burst too, for they have never been heard of since.

As for the Prince and his bride, they released the Christian folk who were imprisoned within the castle; and they took with them as much gold and silver as they could carry, and moved far away from the castle which lay East of the Sun and West of the Moon.

King Valemon,
the White Bear

A NORWEGIAN FOLKTALE

Chapter One
The Golden Wreath

O nce upon a time, there was, as well there might be, a King. He had two daughters, who were ugly and unkind, but the third was as pure and gentle as a clear day, and the King and everyone loved her. She once dreamed of a golden wreath, which was so magnificent that she could not live unless she came into possession of it. But when she could not get it, she became miserable and could not speak for sorrow.

When the King learned that it was the wreath she grieved over, he sent out messengers to the goldsmiths in every land, with a pattern cut just like the one the Princess had dreamt of, and asked them if they could make it.

So the goldsmiths worked both day and night, but some of the wreaths she threw away, and the others she would not so much as look at.

Then one day, when she was in the woods, she saw a White Bear, which had the wreath she had dreamt of between its paws and was playing with it. And she wanted to buy it.

"No," said the White Bear, "it is not for sale for money, but you may have it in return for yourself."

"Well," she said, "life is not worth living without it." It did not matter to her where she went or who she was with, so long as she gained possession of the wreath.

They then agreed that he would fetch her in three days' time, which was a Thursday.

When she came home with the wreath, everyone was delighted because she was happy again, and the King was convinced that it would not be too dangerous a task to keep a White Bear at bay.

On the third day, the entire army was posted round the castle to withstand him. But when the White Bear came, no one could stand against him, for no weapon was capable of harming him, and he knocked them down right and left, so that they lay in heaps.

To the King, this was proving to be an absolute disaster; so he sent out his eldest daughter, and the White Bear settled her upon his back and set off with her.

When they had travelled far, and farther than far, the White Bear asked, "Have you ever sat so softly? Have you ever seen so clearly?"

"Yes," she said. "On my mother's lap, I sat more softly, and in my father's courtyard, I saw more clearly."

"Well," said the White Bear, "you are not the right one then;" and with that, he chased her back home.

The next Thursday, he came again, and things went just the same as they had done before. The army was out with orders to withstand the White Bear, but neither iron nor steel harmed him, so he mowed them down like grass, until the King had to ask him to stop. He then sent out his second-oldest daughter, and the White Bear settled her upon his back and set off with her.

When they had travelled far, and farther than far, the White Bear asked, "Have you ever sat so softly? Have you ever seen so clearly?"

"Yes," she said. "In my father's courtyard, I saw more clearly, and in my mother's lap, I sat more softly."

"Well, you are not the right one then either," said the White Bear, chasing her home as well.

On the eve of the third Thursday, he returned. Then he fought even harder than the other times, until the King thought, *I cannot let him knock down the entire army*, and so he gave him his third daughter in the name of God.

The White Bear then settled her on his back and travelled far, and farther than far, and when they had gone deep into the woods, he asked, as he had asked the others, "Have you ever sat so softly? Have you ever seen so clearly?"

"No, never," she said.

"Ah!" he said. "You are the right one."

They then came to a castle, which was so magnificent that, in comparison, the castle her father resided in was akin to the roughest of homesteads. There she was to stay, and live happily, and she was to have nothing else to do but make sure the fire never went out. The White Bear was away during the day, but at night he was with her, and then he was a man.

Chapter Two
On the Trail of Valemon

For three years, everything was well and good. But every year the Princess had a child, and he took it away with him as soon as it came into the world. She then became more and more upset and depressed, and so she asked the White Bear, "Will you allow me to go home and see my parents?"

"Yes," he said, "I have no objection to that, but first you must promise that you will listen to what your father has to say, not to what your mother would have you do."

She then went home, and when they were alone with her, and she told them how she was faring, her mother wanted to give her a candle so she could see what the White Bear looked like when he turned into a man at night.

But her father said, "No, you should not do that. It will only do more harm than good."

But no matter how it was or not, she brought the candle stub with her when she travelled; and the first thing she did, when he had fallen asleep, was to light it and shine it on him. He was so handsome that she thought, *I can never get my fill of looking at him.* But as she shone the light, a hot drop of tallow dripped onto his forehead, and he woke up.

"What have you done?" he asked. "Now you have made us both unhappy. There was little more than a month left. Had you only endured it, I would have been saved, for there is a Troll hag who has cursed me, so that I am a White Bear in the daytime. But now it is all over with us. Now, I have to go there and take her as my wife."

The Princess cried and carried on, but he had to leave, and leave he would. So she asked, "Might I be able to go with you?"

"No," he said. "That is out of the question."

But as he set off in his bearskin, she grabbed hold of his fur anyway, flung herself onto his back, and held on tight. They then went over mountains and hills, through groves and thickets, until her clothes were torn from her, and she was so deathly tired that she let go of her hold, and knew no more.

When she awoke, she was in a large forest, and so she set out on her way again, but she did not know where the path led.

At long last, she came to a cabin, inside which there were two women, an old woman and a beautiful young girl.

The Princess asked, "Have you seen anything of King Valemon, the White Bear?"

"Yes, he hurried by here early this morning," the young girl said.

"But he was moving so fast," said the old woman, "you will almost certainly never be able to catch up with him."

The young girl ran about, and clipped and played with a pair of golden scissors, which were such that ribbons of silk and strips of velvet flew about her if she but clipped in the air. Wherever the scissors were, something to wear was never lacking.

"But this woman, who has to journey so far and on such rough roads, she will have a hard time of it," said the young girl. "She has more need of these scissors than I," she added, "to be able to cut clothes for herself." She then asked permission to give the Princess the scissors.

"Yes," said the old woman. "Of course, you may."

So the royal traveller journeyed through the forest, to which there seemed to be no end, both day and night, and the next morning, she came to another cabin. Here there were also two women, an old woman and a young girl.

"Good day," said the Princess. "Have you seen anything of King Valemon, the White Bear?" she asked.

"Are you, perhaps, the one who should have had him?" said the old woman.

"Yes, I am."

"He hurried by here yesterday," she said, "but he was moving so fast, you will almost certainly never be able to catch up with him."

The young girl was playing about on the floor with a bottle, which was such that it poured out whatever refreshment anyone wished to drink. Wherever the bottle was, something to drink was never lacking.

"But this woman, who has to journey so far and on such rough roads, she will be thirsty and suffer many more hardships," said the young girl. "She has more need of this bottle than I," she added, then asked permission to give the Princess the bottle.

"Yes," said the old woman. "Of course, you may."

So the royal traveller received the bottle with thanks and set off again, journeying through the same forest, both that day and night.

On the third morning, she came to a cabin, and

here there was also an old woman and a young girl.

"Good day," said the Princess.

"Good day to you," said the old woman.

"Have you seen anything of King Valemon, the White Bear?" she asked.

"Are you, perhaps, the one who should have had him?" said the old woman.

"Yes, I am."

"He hurried by here yesterday," she said, "but he was moving so fast, you will almost certainly never be able to catch up with him."

The young girl was playing on the floor with a tablecloth, which was such that whenever anyone said to it, 'Tablecloth, spread yourself out and cover yourself with the best of dishes,' it did so, and wherever the cloth was, something to eat was never lacking.

"But this woman, who has to journey so far and on such rough roads, she may yet starve and suffer many more hardships," said the young girl. "She has more need of this cloth than I," she added, then asked permission to give the Princess the cloth.

"Yes," said the old woman. "Of course, you may."

So the royal traveller accepted the tablecloth and said her thanks, then she set off. She journeyed far, and farther than far, through the same dark forest, all that day and night.

In the morning, she came to a mountain ridge, which was as steep as a wall, and so high and so wide that she could see no end to it. There was a cabin there too, and when she set foot inside it, the first thing she said was: "Good day. Have you seen if King Valemon, the White Bear, has travelled this way?"

"Good day to you," said the woman. "Are you, perhaps, the one who should have had him?" she asked.

"Yes, I am."

"He set off up the mountain here three days ago," she said, "but nothing which cannot fly can get up there."

The cabin was full of young children, and they all clung to their mother's skirt, crying for food. The woman then put on the fire a pot full of round pebbles.

"What is that good for?" asked the Princess.

"We are so poor," said the woman, "that we have neither food nor clothing, and it is so painful to hear the children crying for a bite of something to eat. But when I put the pot on the fire and say, 'The apples will be cooked soon,' it is as if it dulls their hunger, and they can withstand the pangs for a while longer."

As one can imagine, it was not long before the Princess brought out the tablecloth and the bottle, and when the children were full and happy, she cut out clothes for them with the golden scissors.

"Well," said the woman of the house, "since you have been so profoundly kind to me and my children, it would be a shame if we did not do all we can to try and help you get up the mountain.

"My husband is truly a master blacksmith, one of the best in the world, so you just settle down and rest until he comes home. Then I shall have him forge you claws for your hands and feet, and then you can attempt the climb up the mountain.".

Chapter Three
Lifting the Curse

When the blacksmith returned home, he started work on the claws right away, and the next morning, they were ready.

The Princess had no time to wait, so she thanked them and fastened the steel claws on her hands and feet. Using the steel claws, she crept and crawled up the mountainside all day and night. And when she was so tired that she thought, *I can scarcely lift a hand or foot and will now drop back down to the ground*, she reached the top.

At the top she found a plain, with fields and meadows, so big and broad, she never imagined there could be any land so wide and so flat, and close by there was a castle full of workers of all kinds, who toiled away like ants on an anthill.

The Princess wondered what was going on,

and she soon learned that the Troll hag who had cursed King Valemon, the White Bear, lived here, and in three days, she was going to wed him.

"Might I be able to speak with her?" she asked.

The answer was always the same: "No, that is quite impossible."

So, the Princess sat down beneath the window and started to clip in the air with the golden scissors, so that silk and velvet clothes flew about in all directions like a flurry of snow.

When the Troll hag caught sight of it, she wanted to buy the scissors. "No matter how much the tailors toil away, it does not help," she said, "for there are too many in need of clothes."

"They are not for sale for money," said the Princess, "but you can have them, if I am allowed to sleep with your bridegroom tonight."

"Yes, you can certainly do that," said the Troll hag, "but I will lull him to sleep and awaken him."

When King Valemon had gone to bed, the Troll hag gave him a sleeping draught so he was not able to awaken, for all that the Princess shouted and cried.

The next day the Princess sat beneath the window again and started to pour a drink from the bottle. It flowed like a stream, with beer and with wine, and it never ran dry.

When the Troll hag caught sight of it, she

wanted to buy the bottle. "No matter how much they strive to brew and distil, it does not help," she said, "for there are too many in need of refreshment."

"It is not for sale for money," said the Princess, "but if I am allowed to sleep with your bridegroom tonight, then you shall have it."

"Yes, you can certainly do that," said the Troll hag, "but I will lull him to sleep and awaken him."

When King Valemon had gone to bed, the Troll hag gave him another sleeping draught, so that the night reflected the one before—he did not awaken, no matter how much the Princess shouted and cried.

But that night, one of the craftsmen was working in the room next to that of King Valemon. He heard the crying in there and knew how things stood, and the next day, he told King Valemon, "She must have come, the Princess who is to save you."

That day it was the same story with the tablecloth as with the scissors and the bottle; and when it was dinner time, the Princess went outside the castle, shook out the cloth and said, "Tablecloth, spread yourself out and cover yourself with the best of dishes." There then appeared food, enough for a hundred men, but the Princess sat down to the table alone.

When the Troll hag caught sight of it, she wanted to buy the tablecloth. "No matter how much they cook and roast, it does not help," she said, "for there are too many in need of food."

"It is not for sale for money," said the Princess, "but if I am allowed to sleep with your bridegroom tonight, then you shall have it."

"Yes, you can certainly do that," said the Troll hag, "but I will lull him to sleep and awaken him."

When King Valemon had gone to bed, the Troll hag came in with the sleeping draught, but this time he was watchful for deceit and he duped her. But the Troll hag did not trust him for all that, for she took a darning needle and stuck it into his arm to see if he was truly sound asleep.

But even though it hurt, King Valemon did not move, and so the Princess was allowed to come inside to see him.

Then everything was soon set right between them, and if they could only get rid of the Troll hag, he would be saved. So he got the carpenters to make a trapdoor in the bridge over which the bridal procession had to pass, for it was the custom there that the bride rode at the head of the procession with her friends.

After the Troll hag started across the bridge, the trapdoor opened beneath the bride and all the Troll hags who were her bridesmaids. Then

King Valemon and the Princess, and all the rest of the wedding guests, returned to the castle, and they took as much of the Troll hag's gold and money as they could carry. They then departed for his country to hold their real wedding.

But on the way, King Valemon stopped by the cabins and collected the three young girls, and now the Princess learned why he had taken her babies away from her—it was so that they could help her in finding him. They then drank to their wedding with an ale that was both stiff and strong.

About the Adapter

Rachel Louise Lawrence is a British author who translates and adapts folk and fairy tales from original texts and puts them back into print, particularly the lesser-known British & Celtic variants.

Since writing her first story at the age of six, Rachel has never lost her love of writing and reading. A keen wildlife photographer and gardener, she is currently working on several writing projects.

Why not follow her?

 /Rachel.Louise.Lawrence

 @RLLawrenceBP

 /RLLawrenceBP

/RachelLouiseLawrence

Or visit her website:
www.rachellouiselawrence.com

Other Titles Available

Madame de Villeneuve's
THE STORY OF THE BEAUTY AND THE BEAST
The Original Classic French Fairytale

Story by Gabrielle-Suzanne Barbot de Villeneuve
Translated by James Robinson Planché
Adapted by Rachel Louise Lawrence

Think you know the story of 'Beauty and the Beast'? Think again! This book contains the original tale by Madame de Villeneuve, first published in 1740, and although the classic elements of Beauty giving up her freedom to live with the Beast, during which time she begins to see beyond his grotesque appearance, are present, there is a wealth of rich back story to how the Prince became cursed and revelations about Beauty's parentage, which fail to appear in subsequent versions.

ISBN-13: 978-1502992970

CENDRILLON AND THE GLASS SLIPPER

Story by Charles Perrault
Translated by Rachel Louise Lawrence
Illustrated by Arthur Rackham

*Her godmother, who was a fairy, said,
"You would like to go to the ball, is that not so?"*

When her father remarries, his daughter is mistreated and labelled a Cindermaid by her two new stepsisters. However, when the King's son announces a ball, Cendrillon finds her life forever changed by the appearance of her Fairy Godmother, who just might be able to make all her dreams come true...

ISBN-13: 978-1546510192

ALADDIN AND THE WONDERFUL LAMP
A Classic Folktale from the 'Arabian Nights'

Story by Antoine Galland and Hanna Diyab
Translated by Richard Francis Burton and John Payne
Adapted by Rachel Louise Lawrence

Scarce had Aladdin's mother begun to rub the Lamp when there appeared to her one of the Jinn, who said to her in a voice like thunder, "Say what you want of me. Here am I, your slave and the slave of whosoever holds the Lamp."

One of the most famous tales of the *Arabian Nights*, the story of Aladdin tells of a poor young man who, under false pretences, is recruited by a Magician from the Maghreb to retrieve a Wonderful Lamp from within an Enchanted Treasury. Double-crossed and trapped in an underground cave, Aladdin's future looks bleak until he encounters his first Jinni, after which his life will never be the same again...

ISBN-13: 978-1092815475

SNOW WHITE

Story by Jacob and Wilhelm Grimm
Translated by Rachel Louise Lawrence
Illustrated by Franz Jüttner

*"Mirror, mirror on the wall,
Who in this land is fairest of all?"*

The most famous of the Brothers Grimm fairy tales, *Snow White* is the story of a girl—as white as snow, as red as blood, and as black as ebony—who is the victim of a jealous Queen. But, with the help of seven dwarfs, she might just be able to live happily ever after...

ISBN-13: 978-1522724735

Printed in Great Britain
by Amazon